Ladybird Readers

How many, Spot?

Notes to teachers, parents, and carers

The **Ladybird Readers** Beginner level helps young language learners to become familiar with key conversational phrases in English. The language introduced has clear real-life applications, giving children the tools to hold their first conversations in English.

This book focuses on asking and responding to the question "How many?" and provides practice of numbers 1 to 5 in English. The pictures that accompany the text show a shop setting, which may be used to introduce one or two pieces of topic-based vocabulary, such as "apples" and "lemons" if the children are ready.

There are some activities to do in this book. They will help children practice these skills:

 Listening    Speaking   Reading

LADYBIRD BOOKS

UK | USA | Canada | Ireland | Australia | India | New Zealand | South Africa

Ladybird Books is part of the Penguin Random House group of companies whose addresses can be found at global.penguinrandomhouse.com.
www.penguin.co.uk   www.puffin.co.uk   www.ladybird.co.uk

Penguin
Random House
UK

Text adapted from *Spot Goes Shopping* by Eric Hill, first published by Puffin Books 2014
This version first published by Ladybird Books 2018
001

Copyright © the Eric and Gillian Hill Family Trust, 2018
The moral right of Eric Hill has been asserted

Printed in China
A CIP catalogue record for this book is available from the British Library

ISBN: 978-0-241-31944-4

All correspondence to
Ladybird Books
Penguin Random House Children's
80 Strand, London WC2R 0RL

MIX
Paper from responsible sources
FSC® C018179
www.fsc.org

How many, Spot?

Series Editor: Sorrel Pitts
Based on the story by Eric Hill

"How many apples, Spot?"
"One!"

"How many lemons, Spot?"

"Two!"

"How many boxes, Spot?"

"Three!"

"How many tomatoes, Spot?"
"Four!"

11

"How many oranges, Spot?"

"Five!"

Your turn!

1 **Talk with a friend.**

How many apples?

One!

How many oranges?

Five!

2 **How many? Listen. Circle the numbers.**

1   🍎   (one)   three

2   one   five

3   three   two

4   four   two

Beginner

How are you, Spot?

978–0–241–31941–3 ☐

Yes please, Spot!

978–0–241–31942–0 ☐

How many, Spot?

978–0–241–31944–4 ☐

My name is Spot!

978–0–241–31609–2 ☐